TRANQUILIZERS AND DEPRESSANTS
AFFECTING LIVES

BY HEIDI AYARBE

MOMENTUM

Published by The Child's World®
1980 Lookout Drive • Mankato, MN 56003-1705
800-599-READ • www.childsworld.com

Photographs ©: iStockphoto, cover, 5, 6; Igor
Stevanovic/Shutterstock Images, 8; Shutterstock
Images, 9, 14, 18, 20, 27; Fat Camera/iStockphoto,
10; Switlana Symonenko/Shutterstock Images,
12; Torwai Studio/Shutterstock Images, 16;
Yacob Chuk/iStockphoto, 21; Vlasov Yevhenii/
Shutterstock Images, 22; Cristina Jurca/
Shutterstock Images, 24; Wave Break Media/
Shutterstock Images, 28

ISBN 9781503844896 (Reinforced Library Binding)
ISBN 9781503846487 (Portable Document Format)
ISBN 9781503847675 (Online Multi-user eBook)
LCCN 2019957769

Printed in the United States of America

Some names and details have been changed
throughout this book to protect privacy.

CONTENTS

MOMENTUM

FAST FACTS

What They Are

► Tranquilizers, sedatives, and depressants are called Central Nervous System (CNS) depressants because they slow down brain activity. When brain activity slows down, the body relaxes.

► Some common CNS depressants are Xanax, Valium, and Ambien.

► Common street names for CNS depressants include X, candy, downers, red birds, tranks, yellow jackets, and zombie pills.

How They're Used

► CNS depressants usually come in the form of a pill or liquid. Doctors might **prescribe** them for people who have anxiety disorders, sleep disorders, or panic attacks to help them relax.

► Some people misuse CNS depressants. They might crush pills into powder and snort (or sniff) them into their nose. People also mix CNS depressants with other substances, such as alcohol.

Symptoms of Tranquilizer and CNS Depressant Addiction

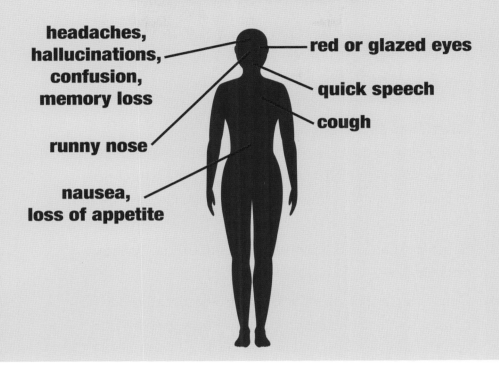

headaches, hallucinations, confusion, memory loss

red or glazed eyes

quick speech

cough

runny nose

nausea, loss of appetite

Physical Effects

► CNS depressants cause drowsy and calming effects. This makes them helpful for sleep disorders and anxiety.

► Short-term side effects include slurred speech, dizziness, shallow breathing, clumsiness, and sleepiness.

► Long-term use can increase breathing problems. It can also lead to **addiction** and cause death.

Mental Effects

► People may experience confusion and have trouble concentrating.

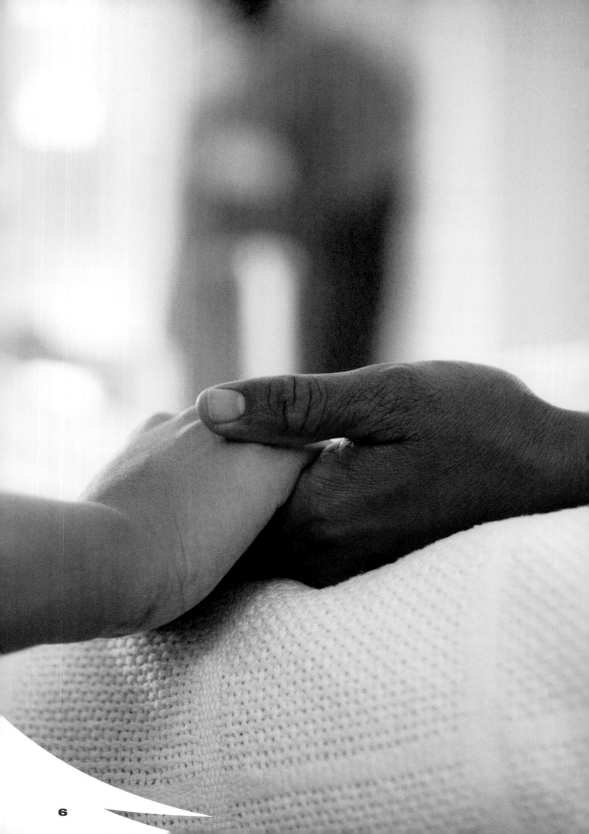

CHAPTER ONE

THE HOSPITAL ROOM

Mariana pulled the hard hospital chair next to her sister's bed. Machines beeped and their lights blinked. Mariana looked at Sara and hardly recognized her. She cupped Sara's hand in hers and wiped away a tear.

The night before, Sara looked so happy. She was excited to go out with friends. Since Sara was 17, most of her friends could drive. She and three other friends piled into a classmate's car to go to a party. Mariana sat on the sofa and looked out the window, watching them drive away. She wished she could join them, but Sara said she was too young. In just two years, Mariana would be 17. But sometimes Mariana wondered if parties weren't that fun.

A few times, Sara had come home from parties acting strange. She stumbled and fell up the stairs to her bedroom. She also talked differently. Her words slurred, or ran together.

◄ **When someone takes too many depressants, he or she could stop breathing and end up in the hospital.**

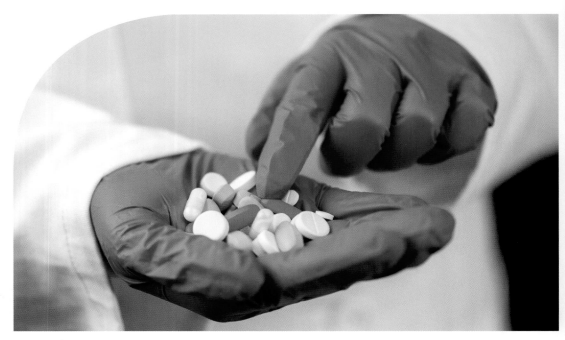

▲ **Tranquilizers and depressants are often colorful pills.**

Mariana once caught Sara and a couple of her friends taking pills before a party. Sara called them "candy." Sara had made Mariana promise not to tell their parents about the pills. She told her sister not to worry. She said it was prescription medication, and that made it OK to take.

That morning, Mariana had found Sara lying on her messy bedroom floor. Mariana shook her, but Sara wouldn't wake up. Mariana raced to tell their mother. Soon, an ambulance came blaring down the street and took Sara to the hospital.

When they got to the hospital, the doctors said that Sara was in a coma. She might not become conscious for a long time. She could even die. If Sara woke up, she might have brain damage.

▲ **When someone has overdosed, he or she has taken too many drugs and needs medical attention.**

The doctor said Sara had **overdosed**. She took too many CNS depressants mixed with alcohol. The combination had slowed down Sara's breathing too much. Less oxygen reached her brain. This is called hypoxia.

Mariana brushed a strand of hair from her sister's face. Sara looked pale. She was hooked up to machines that kept her heart beating. Mariana squeezed Sara's hand. She remembered that Sara had told her to keep quiet about the pills. Mariana said that pharmacies didn't sell drugs that could hurt somebody. She said they weren't like the drugs they learned about in school.

▲ **Social workers help people whose family members are addicted to drugs.**

But Mariana knew that was a lie now. Mariana wished she hadn't ignored that sick feeling in her stomach when she caught Sara with the pills. She had kept Sara's secret, but now Sara could die. A tear dripped down Mariana's face. She felt like this was all her fault.

Mariana heard muffled voices in the hallway. Her mom and dad walked in with a woman, who pulled up a chair and introduced herself as the hospital social worker. The woman said she worked with people who misused drugs. She told Mariana that she would get Sara and the whole family the help they needed.

A knot blocked Mariana's throat. Mariana blurted out that she was sorry and what happened to Sara was all her fault. She told everyone that she had known about the pills.

The social worker told Mariana that many teens believe prescription and over-the-counter medications are safe. But this was untrue. She squeezed Mariana's hand and told her it was nobody's fault. The whole family would get the help and education they needed.

PRESCRIPTION MEDICATIONS

Many teens think that using prescription medication is safe. When prescribed by a doctor, tranquilizers, sedatives, and anxiety medication can be helpful. But when people misuse CNS depressants, it's very dangerous. One in five teens say they have taken someone else's prescription medication. Some steal prescription depressants from family members or get them at parties. Some teens believe prescription depressants are not addictive and therefore they are OK to use, even when the prescription is not for them. Not understanding the dangers puts them at risk for addiction and overdosing.

CHAPTER TWO

WAITING FOR MOM

Ian's alarm blared. He got out of bed and shivered in the cold morning air. The house was quiet except for the clanking sound of the furnace. He felt a burst of excitement. Today was his sixth-grade concert. He woke up his seven-year-old sister, Becca. He helped her get ready for school. Then, Ian made their breakfast, packed their lunches, and braided Becca's hair while they watched cartoons. He made sure to keep the volume down so his mom could rest a while longer.

Ian's mom had a good job. She was a lawyer and worked hard. Sometimes she had trouble sleeping. A doctor prescribed her tranquilizers. When she first started to take her medicine, she seemed more relaxed. She even started to smile more.

But over the last few months, Ian's mom started to act differently. She spent more time at work and returned home late.

◄ **Kids whose parents have an addiction might have to take care of themselves.**

▲ **Tranquilizers may make someone fall asleep more quickly.**

Ian's mom told him she was doing well at work. But his mom often forgot her purse and lunch at home. She even forgot to buy a present for Becca's birthday that month. Ian and Becca relied on their mom to take them to music lessons and soccer practices. But now she always arrived late. They missed doing puzzles and playing games with their mom at night.

At night, Ian's mom took her pills and fell asleep. She woke up cranky many mornings.

Ian told his mom he was worried the pills were changing her behavior. His mom explained she needed the medicine for now, but she could stop anytime. She told Ian not to worry.

His mom assured him all lawyers took these pills. Ian thought she might be lying.

An alarm blared and told Ian it was almost time to go to the bus stop. He knocked on his mom's bedroom door and cracked it open. She sat up in bed as Ian poked his head into the room. She looked sick. Mornings always seemed to be hard for her, but Ian didn't know why.

Ian brought his mom a glass of juice and started the coffee maker. Then, he put a flyer for his school concert next to her mug and underlined the time. Ian and Becca said goodbye. Ian reminded his mom about his concert. The teacher had picked him to sing a song by himself. His mom promised she wouldn't miss it. She told him she would leave work to get there, and after school they could go get hot chocolate. Ian's heart soared with hope.

During health class that day, Ian found a book about drugs. He learned how quickly people can get addicted to prescription medication like the kind his mother took. He also read that people who use drugs can go through **withdrawal** if their body doesn't get the drugs they are addicted to. Ian thought maybe that was why his mother looked sick in the mornings.

The bell rang and students filled the halls. The last class of the day was starting. Ian went to the gym for the music concert.

▲ **Withdrawal usually makes people feel sick.**

Ian looked for his mom in the bleachers full of parents and other family members. He swallowed his disappointment. His mom wasn't there. His teacher, Mr. Jackson, asked about his mom. Ian made an excuse and said she had to work. Mr. Jackson squeezed his shoulder. Ian felt embarrassed and scared. He didn't think anybody would understand what he was going through. Would they judge his mom and his family? He felt so alone.

After the concert, Ian waited for Becca. When he saw his sister, he knew he had to tell her what he thought was happening to their mom. Becca began to cry. Ian tried to comfort her, but he realized they couldn't do this on their own. Instead of going straight home, he told Becca they needed to talk to someone. Ian knocked on Mr. Jackson's door. Together, Becca and Ian told his teacher everything. Mr. Jackson told him he would get them help. Finally, Ian felt less alone.

GETTING HELP FOR FAMILY

Kids with parents who struggle with addiction can reach out to a trusted adult to get help. Teachers, school **counselors**, family members, and coaches are good places to start. There are also **support groups** that help children whose parents are struggling with addiction. Support groups are often led by counselors. Groups can provide support and give hope. They often help others to feel less alone, since many people in the group are experiencing similar situations. Some groups that provide valuable information about addiction include Nar-Anon, Families Anonymous, and Rainbow Days. For emergencies, people can call the Substance Abuse and Mental Health Services (SAMHSA) national hotline at 1-800-662-HELP (4357)

CHAPTER THREE

UNRECOGNIZABLE

Jaden's body started to tingle. Cold sweat beaded at his temples. He gasped for air. Jaden's heart raced, and he felt dizzy. It felt like something was squeezing his chest. Jaden thought he was going to die. It only lasted a few minutes, but it felt like forever. When the fear passed, Jaden was exhausted. He didn't understand why he had felt like that. He was only 14. He thought it wouldn't happen again, but a few weeks later, it did.

Jaden told his parents what was happening to him. His parents took him to visit a doctor. The doctor explained that he was having panic attacks. This meant Jaden was experiencing intense fear without a reason. The doctor said Jaden could deal with the attacks through counseling and medication. The doctor prescribed Jaden CNS depressants. Jaden's parents looked worried. They knew CNS depressants could be addictive.

◄ When someone has a panic attack, he or she may feel like it's hard to breathe.

▲ **Doctors may prescribe CNS depressants to someone who experiences anxiety.**

But the doctor said the medication would be helpful if Jaden used it as prescribed. This meant he shouldn't take more pills than needed.

Jaden worried the attacks would happen during school or while he played in a basketball game. When he had a panic attack, he couldn't control his body. It could be embarrassing if Jaden's classmates saw one of his attacks. Worrying about another panic attack made him feel even more anxious. He started taking extra pills, even though the doctor said not to.

▲ **When someone is addicted to depressants, he or she might steal to get money for drugs.**

Jaden thought the doctor hadn't given him a high enough dose. Jaden assumed if he took more pills, that would keep his panic attacks away.

But the attacks still came. It seemed like every time Jaden took more pills, he needed more. Jaden was developing a **tolerance** to CNS depressants. At first, he felt relaxed and calm. But after a while, his body got used to the feeling. He needed more medication to get the same effect.

▲ **Drug addiction changes people mentally and physically. They may not recognize who they have become.**

Jaden started to find ways to get more medicine. One time, he told his parents somebody broke into his locker and took his medication. Jaden also lied and told the doctor his family was leaving town for a month so he could get an early refill of pills.

Jaden started to forget to turn in homework. He lied to his parents about his bad grades. He felt angry, sad, and confused all the time. Jaden even stole money from his mom's purse to buy pills from a friend. He just needed to get enough pills until his next prescription could be filled.

One morning, Jaden put on his basketball sweatshirt and tried to ignore the tightening feeling in his chest. He told himself it was normal to be nervous on a big game day. He knew he'd feel better once he took a pill. Jaden went to the bathroom and opened the cabinet to find his medication. But the CNS depressants were gone. He searched through all the cabinets in the house. There were no pills. Fear grew inside Jaden.

When Jaden looked at himself in the mirror, he didn't recognize who he'd become. He was scared because he felt like his body wasn't his anymore. He wanted those pills more than anything else. They had become the most important thing to him. Jaden realized he needed help.

At the game, Jaden found his parents in the crowd. He pulled them aside and told them everything. He was afraid of who he had become. Jaden's parents told him they would get him help. It would be hard, but Jaden hoped one day he would feel like himself again.

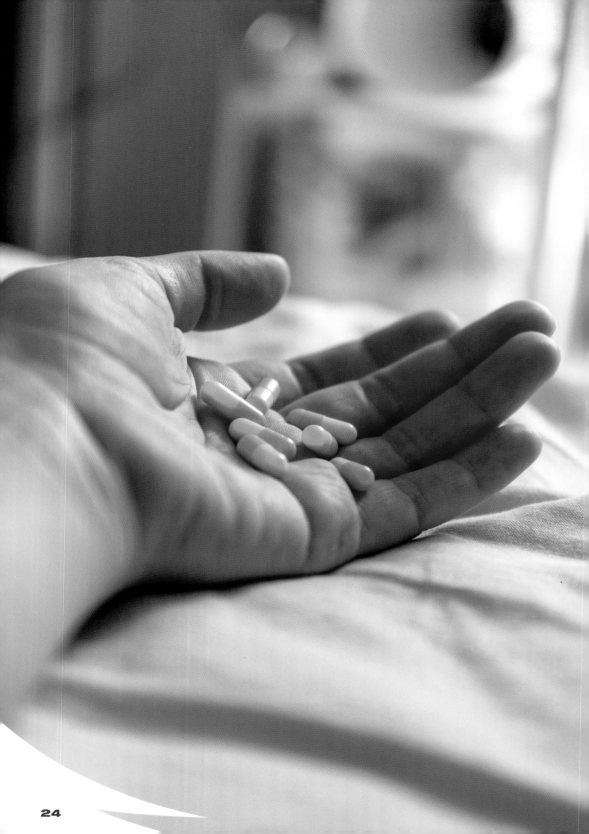

CHAPTER FOUR

GETTING HELP

Kylie felt warm and jittery. Her heart beat quickly in her chest. She rubbed her clammy hands on her jeans and tried to swallow. Her throat was dry and her hands were shaky. The day before, Kylie had run out of her prescription medication. She couldn't ask for more because she'd started taking a higher dose without asking her parents.

Kylie thought she could wait until she got a refill of tranquilizers, but she never expected to feel this bad. Her stomach cramped. She felt hot and sick. Kylie headed to the kitchen to get a drink of water. Suddenly, her vision started to fade and go black.

Kylie woke up in a hospital with a headache. Bright lights glared over her bed. Doctors looked in her eyes with tiny flashlights. Machines with cords were attached to Kylie's arm.

◀ **Taking more CNS depressants than prescribed can make someone really sick.**

Kylie's dad sat beside her bed. He looked afraid, and he wrapped his hand around hers.

The doctors explained that because Kylie was going through withdrawal, she'd had a seizure. This meant Kylie's brain had a sudden disturbance and she lost control of her body. When someone has a CNS depressant addiction, withdrawal symptoms can begin hours after the last drug was taken. Kylie's life was at risk.

The doctors told Kylie she had an addiction. She didn't believe it at first. She explained to them she needed the medicine to help her sleep. She thought since a doctor had prescribed the pills, they had to be good. She didn't believe she was the type of person to have an addiction. She was on the debate team, in all advanced classes, and played volleyball.

Then, Kylie remembered how bad she felt that morning when she'd run out of her medication. She was scared. Her mom and dad wrapped their arms around her. They said they would all get through it together.

It would take time. Kylie first had to go through medical **detox**. This was to make sure Kylie would be safe while her body got rid of the medication. Then, her parents checked her into a drug **rehabilitation** program.

**When someone is experiencing withdrawal ▶
from CNS depressants, he or she can have
a seizure and end up in the hospital.**

▲ Counselors teach people how to cope
with their drug addiction.

During Kylie's time at the rehabilitation clinic, she went to counseling sessions. She learned how to identify triggers, or things that made her want to take the pills. She also learned about healthy coping behaviors. A coping behavior is the way somebody manages stress or anxiety. During her stay at the clinic, she started to exercise, meditate, and keep a journal. She also learned how important it was to eat well and get enough sleep. Kylie lived at the clinic for several weeks during the first phase of her recovery.

After Kylie was released from the clinic, she continued to see counselors to prevent a **relapse**. Kylie had a lot of work ahead of her. She would struggle with addiction for her entire life. To stay healthy, Kylie would need family, counselors, and support groups.

THINK ABOUT IT

► Why do you think doctors prescribe depressants and tranquilizers if people can get addicted to the drugs?
► How do you think people could be unaware that they have an addiction? How can people avoid developing an addiction?
► Why might someone be afraid to tell his or her peers or an adult that a loved one has an addiction?

GLOSSARY

addiction (uh-DIK-shun): An addiction is a very strong need to do or have something regularly. People who feel they need to take CNS depressants may have an addiction.

counselors (KOWN-suh-lurs): Counselors offer advice to someone. Many people with addictions get help from counselors.

detox (DEE-toks): A person who is going through a drug detox has stopped taking the drug. Experiencing a detox can be painful.

overdosed (OH-vur-dohsd): If a person has overdosed, he or she has taken a large amount of a drug and could get sick or die. People who have overdosed on CNS depressants could go into a coma.

prescribe (pri-SKRIBE): Doctors prescribe medication when they write notes that allow a patient to receive treatment. A doctor may prescribe tranquilizers to a person with anxiety.

rehabilitation (ree-uh-bil-uh-TAY-shun): Rehabilitation is a treatment for drug abuse. Most rehabilitation centers have strict rules.

relapse (REE-laps): Relapse occurs when a person who has an addiction had stopped using the drug, but then starts using it again. Kylie wanted to prevent a relapse.

support groups (suh-PORT GROOPS): Support groups are made up of people who come together to share similar experiences. Someone whose parent struggles with addiction can go to support groups.

tolerance (TOL-ur-uhnss): Someone who takes a lot of CNS depressants builds up a tolerance and has to use more to feel their effects. After abusing drugs, he developed a tolerance for them.

withdrawal (with-DRAW-uhl): Withdrawal is the experience of physical and mental effects when a person stops taking an addictive drug. Withdrawal makes it hard for people to stop taking CNS depressants.

TO LEARN MORE

BOOKS

Khanna, Muniya S. *The Worry Workbook for Kids: Helping Children to Overcome Anxiety and the Fear of Uncertainty*. Oakland, CA: New Harbinger Publications, 2018.

Sheff, David. *High: Everything You Want to Know about Drugs, Alcohol, and Addiction*. Boston, MA: Houghton Mifflin Harcourt, 2018.

Small, Cathleen D. *Valium and Other Antianxiety Drugs*. New York, NY: Cavendish Square, 2016.

WEBSITES

Visit our website for links about addiction to depressants and tranquilizers: **childsworld.com/links**

Note to Parents, Teachers, and Librarians: We routinely verify our Web links to make sure they are safe and active sites. So encourage your readers to check them out!

SELECTED BIBLIOGRAPHY

"Prescription CNS Depressants," *National Institute on Drug Abuse*, 6 Mar. 2018, drugabuse.gov. Accessed 20 Jan. 2020.

"Prescription Medicines Are Widely Abused by Teens: Strategies for Parents," *ConsumerMedSafety*, 2015, ConsumerMedSafety.org. Accessed 20 Jan. 2020.

"Teen Addiction Traumatizes Younger Siblings," *Hazelden Betty Ford Foundation*, 2016, hazeldenbettyford.org. Accessed 20 Jan. 2020.

INDEX

ABOUT THE AUTHOR

Heidi Ayarbe is an author, storyteller, and translator. She grew up in Nevada and has lived and traveled all over the world. She now lives in Colombia with her husband and daughters.